For Laura

~ Richard Jones

CATERPILLAR BOOKS

An imprint of the Little Tiger Group

www.littletiger.co.uk

1 Coda Studios, 189 Munster Road, London SW6 6AW

First published in Great Britain 2016

Text by Libby Walden • Text copyright © Caterpillar Books Ltd. 2016

Illustrations copyright © Richard Jones 2016

A CIP Catalogue record for this book is available from the British Library

ISBN: 978-1-84857-508-0

CPB/1800/1039/1018

7 9 10 8 6

Feelings

Illustrated by Richard Jones

Inside my heart and in my head, all kinds of feelings dwell.

As they spark and bounce around I fall under their spell.

Sometimes I want to cry and stomp and really cause a scene

and other times I laugh and smile – what do these feelings mean?

Looking from the outside, I may seem the same as you,

but deep beneath the surface feelings bubble, stir and brew...

Brave

Facing up to all your fears, you scale the mountain top,
and ignore the voice of panic that tries to make you stop.

The journey might be hard and the path may not be straight,

but if you're bold and carry on, the view below looks great!

Sad

With a crash, the river breaks, bursting through its banks;

it happens without warning – no sorry, please or thanks.

It covers every inch of land until there is no more...

just a sea of salty tears with no sign of the shore.

Angry

Deep beneath the surface lies a fire-pit in the ground,

where blazing magma spits and bubbles, swirling all around.

The pressure keeps on mounting and your world begins to shake,

when a sudden, loud eruption forms a scorching lava lake.

Happy

Dancing to the rhythm of a noisy steel-drum band

at a party where the sun beams down and warms the soft white sand.

There's cheerful laughter in the air, the ocean's cool and fine;
the colours of the island glow in the hot sunshine.

Jealous

When someone else has what you want, an emerald mist rolls in.

It churns and seethes and eats you up from somewhere deep within.

Your vision blurs, your mind is fixed on things you do not own
and as green steam begins to rise, you give an envious moan.

Alone

Floating through the turquoise sky in a single bubble,

as though the world has told you off and now you're in deep trouble.

Through the clouds you slowly soar as no one looks or listens,

far away from all the world in a ball that floats and glistens.

Embarrassed

Your face feels like it's burning and the spotlight's shining bright,
the world is staring at you in this pure but blinding light.

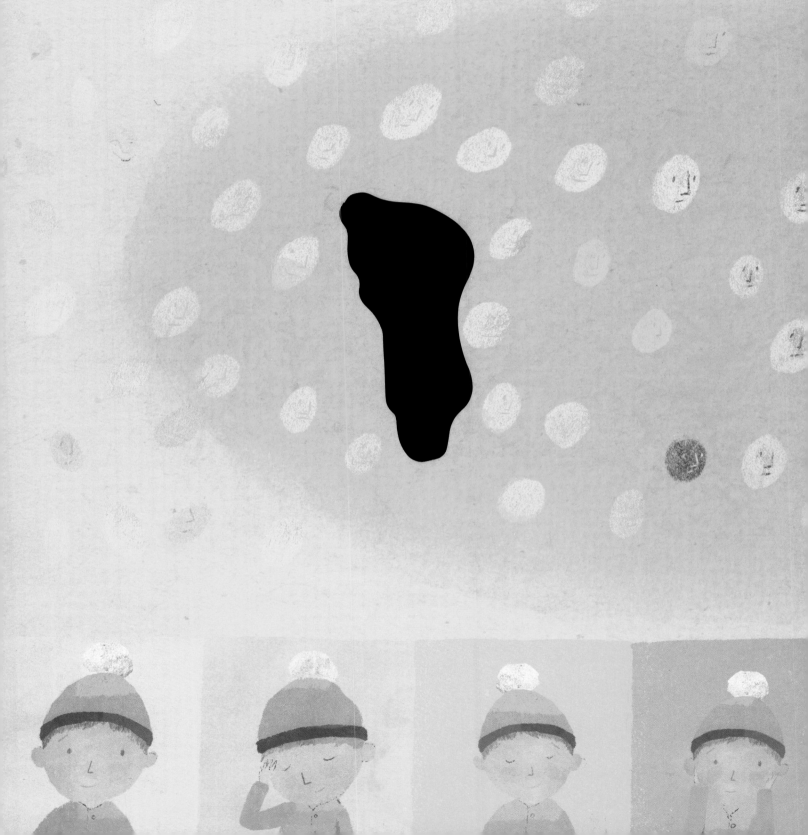

The air is still and silent as your heart beats like a drum;

you wish that you could disappear and all you feel is numb.

Excited

Standing by the bonfire on a chilly autumn night,
waiting for the fireworks to sparkle and delight.

The bright and dazzling colours fizzle, glow and pop
against the darkness of the sky – the explosions are nonstop.

Afraid

Sprinting in between the trees and not sure of your way,

you're being chased by something loud that just won't go away.

Though you keep on running, it follows close behind.

With snapping twigs, it feels so close…or is that in your mind?

Calm

Your little boat floats gently on an ocean smooth and blue,
softly rocking back and forth, you gaze upon the view.

The sea birds serenade you as they slowly pass you by,

and with the lapping of the waves, you give a peaceful sigh.

Everyone is different and their feelings aren't the same
and what you feel is who you are, it's something you must claim.

Try to walk in someone's shoes to see how they might feel.

For though you cannot see them, feelings *are* still strong and real.